About the Book

"Marvelous Marvin's Magical Moment" is a wonderful story about Marvin, a shy, young boy who becomes curiously interested in the wonderful art of magic. Following an opportunity to attend a live magic show and meet the Magician and his magical assistant, Marvin becomes inspired and begins to dream about someday becoming a Magician and performing for an audience in his own magic show. Join Marvin as he takes his classmates on a magical odyssey and develops self-confidence while discovering the meaning of true friendship in the process.

Marvelous Marvin's Magical Moment will leave readers with a sense of joy and encouragement to "dream, believe and reach for the stars!"

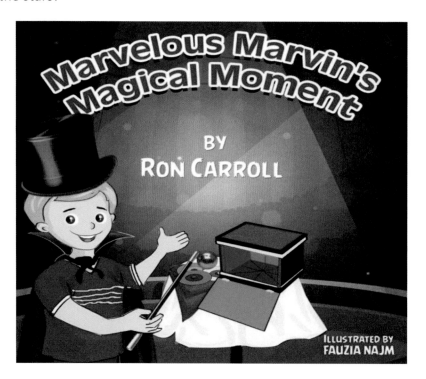

About the Author

Ron Carroll had the opportunity to attend a live magic show at the age of 8, and meet the Magician and his assistant after the show. Ron had been bitten by the "magic bug" and began to learn as much as he could about the art of magic through reading library books, attending magic shows and purchasing magic tricks.

Ron eventually attained amateur and then semi-professional status as a Magician, performing in hundreds of magic shows throughout his life. Ron and his daughter, Tabatha also performed together when she was younger, in a magic and illusion stage show named "Magicana". He has also instructed numerous magic workshops and been a public speaker and mc throughout the years at various events.

Ron resides in the small community of Dillon, Montana where he grew up and has enjoyed two successful careers in both the Montana Army National Guard as well the Montana Youth Challenge Academy. Throughout his life, Ron has been committed to inspiring youth and assisting them to become successful.

<u>Dedications</u>

This book is dedicated to my Mother, LaVerne Carroll.
For always taking the time, leading me by example and showing me unconditional love.

This book is also dedicated to my Daughter, Tabatha Carroll.
For the wonderful memories I will always hold close and for being the magnificent other half of the most dynamic magical duo that once was... MAGICANA!

"Marvelous Marvin's Magical Moment"

Marvin sat at his desk in the classroom, anxiously waiting for the bell. Suddenly, the bell rang and Marvin and his classmates gave a big cheer as they began toward the door.

"Have a good weekend everyone, I will see you all on Monday", said Mrs. Mayberry, Marvin's teacher.

Marvin waited patiently in front of the school for his best friend Maggie.
"Are you ready?" asked Maggie, as she approached Marvin.
"I sure am" said Marvin". And together, they started their short walk home, a walk
they took after school each day

As they began walking, Maggie turned to Marvin and said, "Marvin, did you hear about the Magic Show this weekend?" Maggie knew how much Marvin loved magic. Marvin stopped and looked at Maggie, and with a very excited voice asked, "A magic show? Really? Where? When?" "Tomorrow night, at the high school auditorium. I saw a poster, I'll show it to you on the way home" said Maggie. Maggie led Marvin to the store window where she had seen the poster. The poster read, "The Magic & Illusion of the Amazing Jay".

"WOW! A real magic show, a real Magician",
exclaimed Marvin, as he stared at the poster.

Marvin couldn't wait to get home to tell his mother about the Magic Show.
As Marvin walked into his house, he said with a very loud and very excited voice,
"Mother, mother, there is a Magic Show tomorrow night!
Can I please go, mother, please?" asked Marvin.

With a giggle in her voice, Marvin's mother said, "Of course you can go, Marvin. Your father and I already talked about it and we knew you would be excited. We were going to surprise you at dinner. I will take you to the Magic Show." With that, Marvin's mother reached into her apron pocket, pulled out three tickets and handed them to Marvin. "I got an extra ticket so we can take Maggie with us also. You can tell Maggie after dinner." The colorful tickets read… "The Magic & Illusion of the Amazing Jay"! "Wow! Thank you so much!" said Marvin as he hugged his mother.

At bedtime later that evening, Marvin's mother tucked him into bed. "You need to get some sleep. We have a big day tomorrow!" said Marvin's mother as she leaned over and kissed Marvin on the forehead. "Good night mom. I love you!" said Marvin to his mother. "Good night Marvin. I love you too... very much!" she said to Marvin as she turned off the light. And with that, Marvin drifted off to sleep with happy thoughts of the exciting day that lay ahead.

The next evening, Marvin, his mother and Maggie arrived at the auditorium for the Magic Show. Marvin was thrilled to find that their seats were in the very first row and right in front of the stage. "Do you think we will get to meet the Magician after the show?" asked Marvin. "Perhaps", Marvin's mother replied. Marvin sat with great anticipation for what seemed forever for the Magic Show to begin.

Then, suddenly, the auditorium lights dimmed and mysterious music began to play. The magic show was finally here! At the beginning of the show, The Amazing Jay made his pretty assistant, Tabatha, appear from an empty box on stage and then introduced her to the audience. For the next hour and a half, Marvin watched closely as The Amazing Jay performed impossible feats of magic with his assistant, Tabatha. He made her vanish from a large box only to reappear in the back of the auditorium. Near the end of the show, he made her float in mid-air on stage..

When the magic show was over, Maggie, Marvin and his mother made their way to the lobby of the auditorium to meet the Magician and his Assistant and get their autographs. "What's your name?" asked The Amazing Jay, as he shook Marvin's hand. "I'm Marvin, and I want to be a Magician someday" said Marvin. "Did you enjoy the Magic Show, Marvin?" asked Tabatha. "I sure did, you were both amazing!" said Marvin. The Amazing Jay and Tabatha both autographed his poster. With that, Marvin thanked them again and said goodbye as he, his mother and Maggie walked out of the auditorium.

As soon as Marvin got home, he put his magic poster on his bedroom wall. He couldn't wait to go to school the next week and tell all of his classmates about the magic show. That night, he drifted off to sleep with happy thoughts of the magic show and his dream of becoming a Magician some day.

Monday morning arrived and Marvin and his classmates were back in school. "Marvin, would you like to tell everyone about the Magic Show?" asked Mrs. Mayberry. Marvin was shy, but he replied with an enthusiastic "yes" and walked to the front of the classroom. Marvin began to tell his classmates all about the magic show. They were all amazed to learn that Marvin was able to meet the Magician and his Assistant after the show and get his poster autographed. Marvin told his classmates that he was learning about magic and practicing his magic tricks so that he could be a Magician someday. "That would be wonderful, Marvin, perhaps you can put on a small magic show here in our classroom." said Mrs. Mayberry. After some hesitation, Marvin replied with a nervous "yes".

For the next several weeks, Marvin practiced and rehearsed his magic tricks in front of a mirror. Sometimes, his cat Mittens would sit and watch. With each day and week of practice, Marvin got better and better. His father helped him to build a magician's table and a small vanishing box in his woodshop so that Marvin could vanish his pet hamster Chip at the end of his magic show at school. Although he was still nervous at the thought of performing in front of his class, Marvin was excited about the magic show.

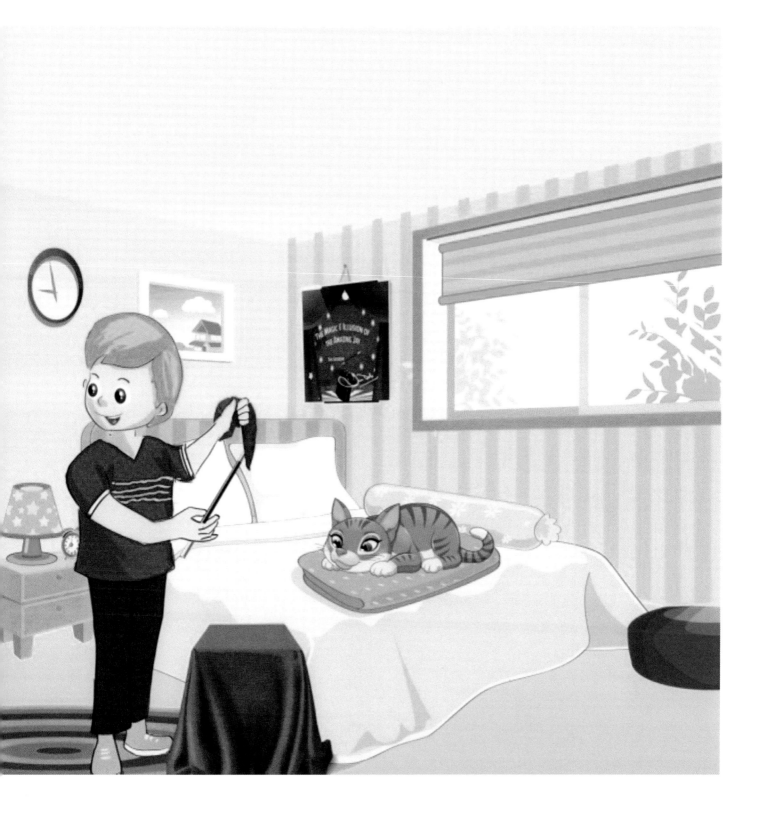

After a few weeks of practicing, Marvin's big magic show was only a day away. Marvin's mother and father sat in the living room and pretended to be his audience as Marvin performed his magic tricks for them. "That was wonderful!" said Marvin's mother. "That was really terrific, we are both very proud of you!" said Marvin's father.

With that, Marvin's mother brought a box into the living room and placed it in front of him. "Open it!" said his mother with a big smile on her face. Marvin loved surprises. What could it be, he wondered to himself. Marvin opened the box and found a black top hat. "Wow! A real magician's top hat" said Marvin. "There's something else in the box" said Marvin's father. Marvin reached back into the box and pulled out a flashy red and black magician's cape. "Wow!" exclaimed Marvin. "I found the top hat at the thrift store and I sewed the cape for you, Marvin", said his mother. Marvin placed the top hat on his head and then flung the cape over his shoulders. "They fit perfect! Thank you both, so much" said Marvin. "Now I just need a stage name" said Marvin. "You'll think of something" said Marvin's mother.

The big day was finally here! It was the final day of school for the year which also meant it was time for Marvin's big Magic Show. Maggie helped Marvin carry his magic props into the classroom and set them up before class started. "I'm kind of nervous", Marvin said to Maggie. "You're going to be great" replied Maggie. "You've practiced, and you are ready!" she said. Then, the morning bell rang and Marvin's classmates took their seats. Mrs. Mayberry walked to the front of the class. "Good morning everyone" she said. "I would like to say thank you to Marvin. I know that he has worked very hard and practiced many hours these past several weeks to get ready for this Magic Show for all of us". With that, she introduced Marvin, who walked to the front of the class as his classmates clapped..

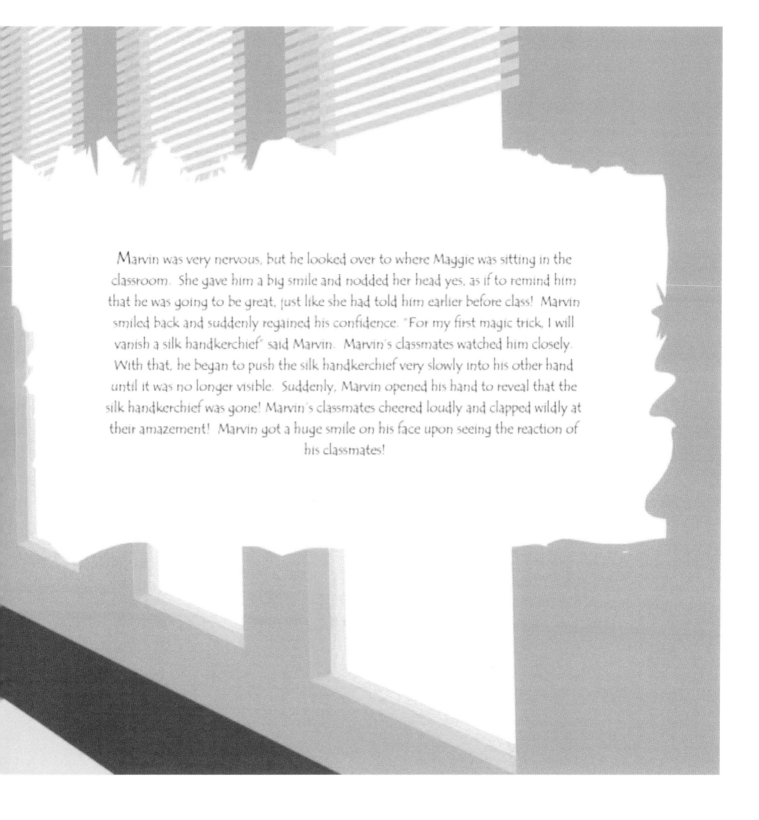

Marvin was very nervous, but he looked over to where Maggie was sitting in the classroom. She gave him a big smile and nodded her head yes, as if to remind him that he was going to be great, just like she had told him earlier before class! Marvin smiled back and suddenly regained his confidence. "For my first magic trick, I will vanish a silk handkerchief" said Marvin. Marvin's classmates watched him closely. With that, he began to push the silk handkerchief very slowly into his other hand until it was no longer visible. Suddenly, Marvin opened his hand to reveal that the silk handkerchief was gone! Marvin's classmates cheered loudly and clapped wildly at their amazement! Marvin got a huge smile on his face upon seeing the reaction of his classmates!

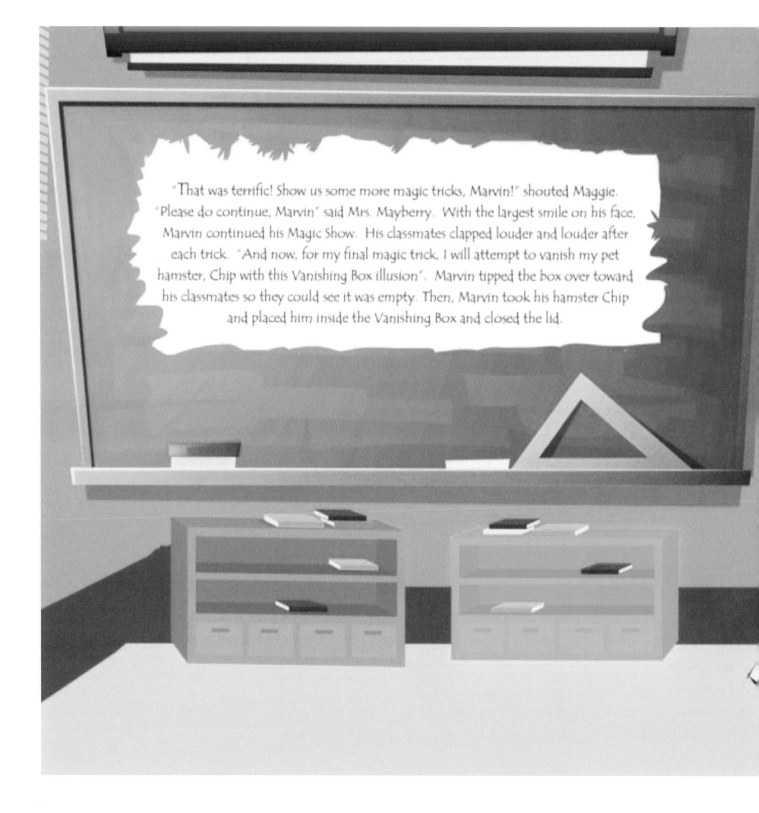

"That was terrific! Show us some more magic tricks, Marvin!" shouted Maggie. "Please do continue, Marvin" said Mrs. Mayberry. With the largest smile on his face, Marvin continued his Magic Show. His classmates clapped louder and louder after each trick. "And now, for my final magic trick, I will attempt to vanish my pet hamster, Chip with this Vanishing Box illusion". Marvin tipped the box over toward his classmates so they could see it was empty. Then, Marvin took his hamster Chip and placed him inside the Vanishing Box and closed the lid.

With a magical pass over the top of the box with his magic wand, Marvin opened the lid and tipped the box back over toward the class to show them that it was empty. Chip the hamster had vanished! Marvin's classmates cheered and clapped wildly at their astonishment! With that, Marvin thanked his classmates for being such a wonderful audience. He also gave a special thanks to his best friend Maggie for believing in him and for being so helpful. He finished by thanking his teacher, Mrs. Mayberry for being so caring and encouraging. He then took a much deserved bow like a real Magician at the end of his show. "That was absolutely marvelous, Marvin" said Mrs. Mayberry. "Marvelous Marvin, that's it, that can be my stage name!" said Marvin.

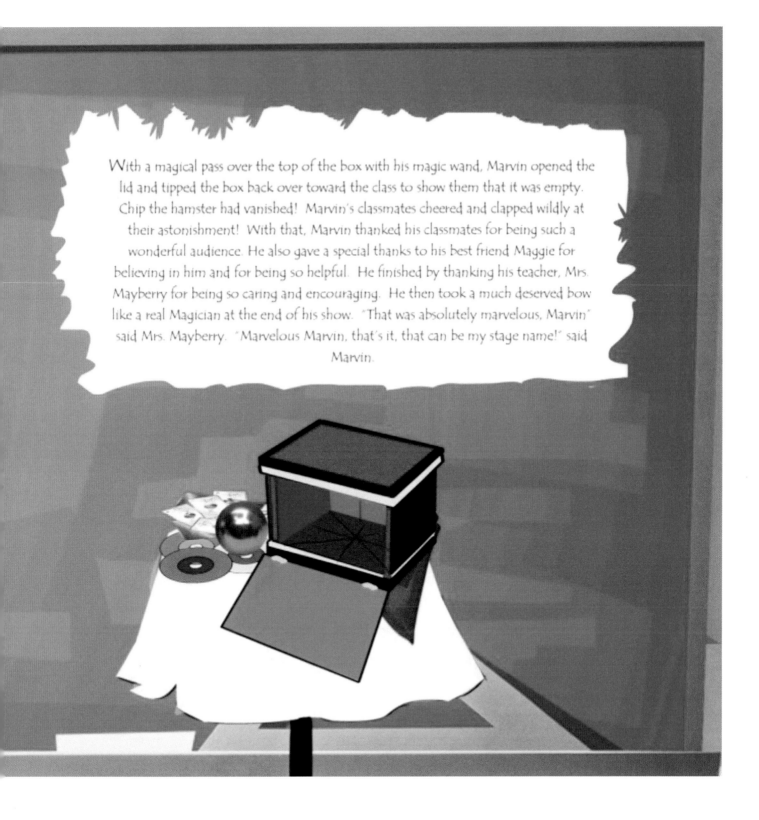

Marvin couldn't wait to get home and tell his mother and father all about his big Magic Show, which he did, along with the wonderful way in which his classmates had enjoyed his performance and clapped for him. That night, Marvin's mother tucked him into bed and said goodnight. Marvin drifted off to sleep, thinking only happy, magical thoughts, knowing that he had finally become a real Magician. After all, he was now…… Marvelous Marvin!

Made in the USA
Middletown, DE
15 June 2020